Blood Bound

Jason Morgan

Published by Jason Morgan, 2022.

BLOOD BOUND

First edition. October 25, 2022.

ISBN: 979-8215508633

Written by Jason Morgan.

Table of Contents

Chapter One.

The electric whirring of a razor wasn't only mentally traumatizing for Gillian but also physically terrifying as the clipper grazed her scalp in more places than one.

Needless to say, her makeshift barber wasn't gentle with her duties, but the least anyone in that room cared about was stellar barbing services. Gillian wasn't sure what would come after the unsolicited shave. Still, she knew it wouldn't be a galore of spa treatments afterward, with the sinister ambiance and the evil couple sharing horrific anecdotes since she came back to consciousness.

Gillian spent the next few minutes mentally cursing herself for not listening to her instincts and just staying the heck away from The Place that evening. She should have just called in sick. It wasn't like The Place was going to miss a stripper on a busy night, but she wanted the extra paper that came with payday tips, which had been the genesis of her life turning upside-down.

The Place was not an establishment one would be proud of associating with, but that had not stopped its patrons from trooping in every night. It didn't take long before the strip club earned its name 'The Place' due to the gossiping wives of its patrons always shying away from calling it the original 'Sin City.' Its patrons were mostly married men ranging from the elite to the once-in-a-blue-moon average men who always frequented there once a month and were too generous with their salaries because they had a reputation to uphold.

The only time women ever managed to sneak past security and maneuver their way into the complex camouflaged stripping arena of The Place. Only when a vengeful wife had been informed of her husband's excesses and could not wait before he finished his business and (or) money before causing a scene. It was the busiest hour of the night; Gillian, along with many occupants in the room, had noticed when Bonnie and Clyde had breezed into The Place hand in hand.

Gillian had initially thought the man had come to pimp off the insanely attractive redhead on his arm, and she had immediately seen the other woman as a threat to her livelihood. Gillian wasn't sure if she was marking her territory or if it was just an involuntary act of jealousy, but she doubled up her efforts and danced like never before. She twisted, turned, and wrapped herself around the pole in ways that would have been unnatural and unattainable, even to her, had she not sniffed out a threat. What made her keep at it for so long was the cheers, wild applause, and several hundred dollar bills being sprayed and thrown into her booth.

Gillian was high on Cloud Nine even after the dance was over. Not only had she shown the redhead who was boss at The Place, but she'd also raked in more than fifteen grand in a single dance, minus the club's commission for the first time since her career began. She'd also gotten several cards from the elite men who seemed to be able to provide upcoming, highly paid, private shows.

Gillian was finally at the peak of her career, and she'd been reveling in it. She'd gotten into her private dressing room when the redhead appeared from nowhere and smacked her naked ass. Not only did Gillian immediately take offense at the assault, but she also felt insulted by the action and immediately wanted to retaliate. However, she was baffled by an irresistible offer the redhead made.

"Fifty grand for a threesome with my man and I tonight," the crazy-looking redhead had said with a knowing smile. It had taken all the restraint Gillian had in her to refuse the offer and tell Bonnie to fuck off. However, she figured the unpleasant expression the redhead's face had morphed into was worth much more than fifty thousand dollars.

Moreover, she would make that amount or even more once she called the numbers on her complimentary cards.

If Gillian had any idea whatsoever, she had made a regret, as the redhead had predicted before vanishing from her dressing room; she would have run after the redhead instead of watching her go and beg for a second chance to redeem herself. However, as the whirring of the electric clipper suddenly stopped, and she was roughly pulled to her feet by the redhead's 'man,' she knew it was already too late to redeem herself, and her only mistake that night was showing up at The Place.

Opposing Gillian's sad conclusion, she wouldn't be heard from again. She made it back to town three days later. But all that remained of her lifeless, hairless, eyeless body was swiftly disintegrating by the shoreline waters, licking away at the body until a set of frolicking teenagers found her on a beach day.

Gillian Dowager was swiftly tagged and announced on live TV by the State Sheriff of the Manhattan Police Department as the fifth victim of The Menace, as the general public had dubbed the serial killer. It wasn't the kind of fame the deceased had in mind when her voodoo prophetess said she should gear up for baffling human popularity, but she was a little too dead to be able to choose her fate.

Ray was having a good day until he wasn't. He'd just returned from his six weeks' leave and felt refreshed. As usual, he had woken up on the right side of his king-size bed. Then he'd pulled apart the curtains of the floor-to-ceiling window in his penthouse apartment to behold the beautiful chaos of the city before going about his rigorous routine, plucking the keys to his power bike from what used to be an ashtray and striding fluently towards the elevator.

Everything went smoothly, riding down the elevator, the ride to his workplace, and even walking into the debriefing about his latest case. The girlish ladies squirmed as he sent his dazzling smiles and winked their way. Troyer, Ray's right-hand techie, looked better than he would typically have on a Monday morning when he stopped by to check on him.

However, sitting before the only woman who was immune to his charms and took great pleasure in rattling him to his core with every case she brought his way, he wished he'd not shown up at work that day. He wished he'd not woken up on that very fateful morning.

"I'm afraid, Liz, I decline—" he began to say, but the perfect thirty-year-old cut right in before he could finish spitting the words out.

"I'm afraid, Ray, we're not being paid to decline cases that need our expertise to handle. The whole of the Manhattan PD is counting on the hotshot investigator that's coming in from the FBI, and I personally do not think there's a better man for the job than you, Ray. No excuses, your chopper leaves by noon."

Ray would have blushed at the fact his iron-lady crush had deemed it fit to compliment him on that morning if he wasn't busy regretting his life choices at that moment. Her conclusion held a tone of finality to it, so Ray knew better than to try reasoning with her after she'd dismissed him.

He stood up and stiffly saluted her before making for the exit in an opposite demeanor to which he'd come in. He stopped right in his tracks when Liz cleared her throat, hoping she miraculously had a rethink and would take back the assignment from him.

"Logan was my first choice and would have been a better match for this case, but Melissa argued without hesitation that it's your hometown and no one else here would know the terrain better than you do. I hope to God that she is right, Ray. You'd better not mess this up..."

Ray resumed his pace and was out of the door before Liz finished talking. From afar, one would think his ego got bruised because he'd once again tagged him as second best to a privileged chino-pants playboy from Elitesville. However, what had Ray's jaw working like a ruminant animal and fist clenching and unclenching as though he was trying to grab hold of the air was his past being so casually mentioned.

It was a past he'd been trying so hard to forget, and Liz was one of the few people who knew. The last thing Ray had expected her to do was to rip the band-aid off old wounds brutally and still have the audacity to sound so lazy about it.

It wasn't only a slap to the face but a challenge to prove to her that he wasn't the street rat she thought him to be. Ray liked her a little less that morning, but his annoyance towards his friend swiftly overcame his dislike for his boss as he approached Melissa's office.

"I thought we talked about your unsolicited interference in Liz's dealings with me, Mel," Ray said in a loud voice as he barged into the spacious office of his friend.

The forty-nine-year-old Black woman was unperturbed by his sudden entrance and outburst. She lazily adjusted her reading glasses and closed the journal she was writing on before even bothering to look up at Ray.

"Well, a lovely morning to you too, my friend." Her sarcasm was clear as day, but Ray barely acknowledged the blow and delved right down to venting.

"There's no way I can have a fair chance with Liz if she keeps thinking you're doing me favors because I'm warming up your bed. Which you and I both know isn't true!"

If Melissa felt slighted by the look of utter disgust with which Ray had delivered his speech, she didn't show it. She just nodded and waited for him to continue. She only spoke up when it was evident he had finished talking.

"You and I know you'll be nowhere close to where you're now without my 'unsolicited interference.'" Melissa barely finished her statement before Ray fiercely replied.

"That is not fucking true, Mel, and you know—"

"Oh, but it is, Ray." The older of the duo was quick to interrupt this time. "Always fighting for one of my own is why a common 'Black receptionist,' much less, would even be considered a part of the SCID in the first place." Melissa's voice wasn't loud when she spoke, but it still matched the fierceness her seemingly ungrateful buddy was currently exhibiting.

There was a cold moment of silence that seemed to last for ages when, in fact, it lasted only ten seconds. When Ray finally spoke, his hurt was obvious in his tone;

"I can't believe you, of all people, don't believe in my capabilities either."

"I do," Melissa replied without missing a beat. "Between you and me, it has been proven beyond any reasonable doubt that you're the best detective we have in the bureau." As she talked, she stood up from her leather chair and began walking towards Ray in deliberately slow steps. "But because people like Liz, who have zero interest in your potential or penis because of your skin color, nepotism has to save your black ass here, and common sense hopefully will save you from being a simpering ninny."

Ray was even more hurt by Melissa's cruelty and speechless because there was no way he could defend himself against the truth.

"You're welcome," The slender woman continued as she finally reached him. Advantaged by her kitten heels, the woman's already intimidating height was almost at his own 6' 4". Even though she was a few inches shorter, Ray felt intimidated by their proximity.

At such a nearness, he could see the weak wrinkles in her seemingly pristine business suit, the silver streaks in Melissa's black curls became clearer, and the wrinkles hiding behind the makeup spoke volumes of her years of experience and wisdom as an executive in the bureau. In her eyes, Ray could see the unadulterated love the woman had for him.

The woman smothered the non-existent wrinkles on his jacket and pulled at his collar in a way that painfully reminded Ray of his mother.

"You know how Liz detests tardiness. I'd invest my time in packing a heavy suitcase for this trip down memory lane if I were you."

With that information said, Melissa patted Ray's shoulder in a way that said 'get out and go make mama proud.' The cunning woman did not have to say anything. Somehow, that was all Ray needed to feel better.

He left the room without another word.

Chapter Two.

Julia Michaelson was very peeved.

First off, she'd been called in too early for an 'official debrief' in the words of McCain, which was as unnecessary as the venue he'd picked for it. There were just four in the conference room at 6 am, and the case wasn't necessarily top secret or high profile. Even if a meeting were a must, Peter's office would have done fine for the meeting.

Julia suspected that the entire meeting and venue were just propaganda and eyeservice in honor of the newest addition to the team. The conference room was one of the coolest rooms the department could boast of, hence the reason they were currently redoing a debriefing they'd done weeks ago in a room that resembled an underpopulated lecture theater.

The newest addition to the team took up the chair two seats away from her and kept swiveling the seat in a very distracting manner, making Julia wonder if swivel chairs were a novelty to him. The idiot seemed unimpressed and bored from the ramblings the Sheriff spewed, and it annoyed her that the unassuming man had put so much effort into the presentation.

She felt like putting a bullet into the skull of the stupid young man. It would be such a waste of toned muscles and a handsome face, but Jules was sure it was all he brought to the table anyway;

All beauty and zero brains.

"It's an honor to have the best of FBI come home to work with us—"

"A serial killer and a duty to my force brought me here. I'm not 'home' to work with anybody," Her boss was blatantly cut off by the new guy, and even though Peter hated being interrupted, Julia watched him swallow up his displeasure as he plastered a wide-grinning smile on his face.

Julia decided then that she wasn't going to like the new guy. "Very well then, we've tried, but woefully failed, to apprehend this criminal—"

While Jules was still fuming that her boss was under-crediting their efforts to gas up a total stranger, the egocentric airhead interrupted the former again.

"Well, I agree that you are failing woefully. Cheers to that." It took all of her restraint to stay in her chair, not reach for the young man, and slap him into a reasonable amount of sensibility.

"Uh... well. We could use your expertise in this case, sir. We're looking forward to you doing your magic, so we can finally put all of these behind us, and you can be on your sweet way back to..."

Peter McCain trailed off awkwardly. Julia was glad he wasn't embarrassing the whole Manhattan Police Department any further. She thought that was the blasted end of the gruesomely annoying meeting until her boss dropped the next bombshell that shook her to the core;

"We're leaving you in charge of overseeing the entire case until it is closed, sir." Jules thought there was a problem with her hearing, but when she heard the arrogant response from the alpha-male wannabe, she could not restrain herself anymore.

"I am sorry about this, Peter, but I beg to differ. It's just not done to put a stranger in charge of a serious case. We do not even know this guy, and it is already evident that any slip-up can discover even more bodies at a faster rate. We cannot afford to trust someone of unknown capabilities with such sensitive responsibility."

Julia was out of breath by the time she finished, but the confused look on her boss's face and the new guy made all the stress worth it. There were several moments of silence in the room after Julia's sudden outburst. However, the first person to recover and dignify her with a response was the person she least expected or appreciated.

"Your concerns are valid, Miss..." the new guy trailed off for Julia to fill in his silence with her name, but Julia didn't care enough to indulge him, so the silence swiftly became an awkwardly long one.

"Well," Ray continued after clearing his throat, "be rest assured that you're in the right hands—"

"With all due respect, I believe the FBI sent us a detective to help out, not to override protocol and take over the case." Julia was quick to cut Ray short with the most passive-aggressive tone she'd ever used in her career.

"Considering that the FBI even sent someone to 'help' out at all just airs your dirty panties of incompetence to the entire state, don't you think?"

"Well, Mr. Big shot, why don't you run this OP on your own, seeing that an entire police department is useless in your books."

"Awfully naive of you to think I can't fish out the killer in five working days with a flashlight and a pocket journal. You really think I got to be the only Black agent in the Special Crimes Intelligence by sleeping with superiors twice my age and throwing tantrums about who to be in charge?"

By the time an amused-looking Ray finished talking, it was evident on her expression that Julia was brewing venomous words to spit back in reply.

Peter knew, by experience, that he had to interfere before Julia opened her mouth again, or they would all regret the outcome. Including Julia.

"It doesn't really matter who's in charge, Jules," Peter spoke in a very uncomfortable tone after a humorless chuckle. "The only thing that absolutely matters is that we catch this killer before another redhead washes up on the bank of another river."

Julia began to reason with her boss's perception and realized she was being selfish. It was more important that the killer was apprehended and safely locked away. Who took charge of the operation was important for her career too, but not more important than the lives that were at stake as their killer still roamed the streets and lurked in the shadows.

"The least I'll settle for is being his partner," Julia conceded. "His equal all through this OP. I won't take orders from him, only suggestions. Anything less than that, I'm out."

To her relief, her boss saw the good in her suggestion and pitched it to the handsome bastard two seats away, who readily agreed.

Julia couldn't believe he had judged her in his mind, found her guilty, and casually proclaimed his verdict while trying to prove a point to her. Such an attitude only belonged to slimy creatures who indulge in something similar to what they were accusing the other party of;

It always took one to know another.

The short, buff sheriff was quick to conclude the meeting for fear another heated, uncontrollable argument would break forth again and was dashing out of the conference room before Julia could say 'Jack.' It didn't take long before Douglas, her previous partner on the case, took to his heels before she could even ask why he'd been awfully silent throughout the meeting.

In less than thirty seconds, she was left alone in the room with the new guy, who did not seem to be in a hurry to let go of his latest discovery, aka the swiveling chair.

Julia began to put the file cases together in haste to get out of the room as fast as possible. She wasn't in the mood for a back-and-forth conversation that would further stretch her already taut nerves.

"I'll need a breakdown of the victims' profiles, Miss Jules. If you would be so kind as to grab coffee with me at lunch, maybe you can introduce me to the details."

Julia couldn't quite believe her ears.

"You've got to be kidding me." Her exasperation was clear as day. "If you'd even paid a little bit of attention towards Peter during the entire meeting, you would have gotten the 'breakdown' you 'needed.'"

"The sheriff isn't the one who begged to be my partner–"

"How dare–"

"Plus, he wasn't the one running the OP before, and he wouldn't have known the intricacies of things you may have omitted in the reports. Those are the details I need."

For a full minute, Julia was speechless.

"If you think you can convince me to have a conversation with you over a blasted cup of coffee, then you have another thing coming," was the best reply she could come up with at that moment.

She was still in utter disbelief that she'd scored herself a prick of all the people available at the FBI. Julia could already feel a headache coming on.

"Well, suit yourself. Don't just go complaining to your sugar daddy about my conduct if I decide to go solo." Julia whirled around so fast that a joint in her neck popped.

"Because I am close to Peter doesn't mean I am sleeping with him, prick! That man is like a father to me, for Pete's sake!"

"I didn't say otherwise," Ray shrugged nonchalantly, "I'm not judging if you're sleeping with him, either. I mean, you both look cute together."

The level at which Julia was now livid would have steam coming out of her ears and nostrils if they were in a cartoon.

"Biased judgment of people's character and being an overall annoying asshole doesn't make for a good detective. It just makes me wonder if you really got to the height you boast so much about, on your own merit, or if some nepotism is in play at your workplace."

Julia didn't think it was possible, but she saw Ray's expression harden as she talked. She knew she had just delivered a low blow to one of his sensitive spots, and she had no regrets about it.

Julia was finishing putting together files and fixing to sashay out of the room with a superior demeanor of a warrior that just conquered a territory. However, what the new guy had to say was enough for her to reconsider.

"I hear the autopsy results for the latest victim are due for delivery today. I say instead of having them delivered, and we go to the lab for collection. I'm sure there are a few remarks we'd get from your plug that are not in the official document. I'd like to see the victim's body myself, in fact."

Julia had to applaud the guy for his thorough thoughtfulness, but only in her head. Visibly, all she did was nod in an aloof manner, unanchored the keys to her patrol vehicle, and flung it his way.

Ray caught the keys in a swift, fluid motion.

"Good thing I'm driving. We're stopping at the nearest Starbucks to get coffee. It's about time to get some caffeine running in my bloodstream."

Julia wasn't pleased about the adamancy, but it was a good start that they could at least have an understanding and be civil with each other when it came to what brought them together in the first place; Work.

The visit to the forensic lab was swift and achieved his purpose. The drive there was mainly silent and left each occupant of the car in their own private thoughts. Julia wondered if the man was always that silent or if it was just a reaction to her earlier accusation that seemed to have hit home so closely.

However, she preferred him when he wasn't stretching her nerve endings to the point of snapping.

He ended up not getting his coffee until after he analyzed the body and conversed at length with Oliver, the technician who'd run the tests on the victim's body.

He was very professional; Julia had to give him that. When he handed her the copy of the autopsy results and informed her he was taking the afternoon off, Julia could detect that the visit had affected him more than he was willing to share.

She wondered why it was so and decided to follow him to satisfy her curiosity.

Chapter Three.

In the two days Ray had made it back to Manhattan, he had been able to make findings about the resting place of his mom. When he realized it was just a short distance from the laboratory he had visited with his pesky little partner, he decided it was finally time to face his past.

Getting rid of the annoying flea who called herself his partner wasn't hard. She was enthusiastic about being rid of him, and he did not spend time dwelling on how he was equally relieved to be away from her.

Ray picked his way toward the cemetery as soon as she drove out of sight. Boroughs' cemetery was within walking distance, so he trekked all the way in a bid to mentally prepare his mind for what he was about to do. He even stopped at the flower shop close to the graveyard to get his mother's favorite flowers to stall the inevitable.

Ultimately, he made his way to the registry, leading to his mother's final resting place in no time.

Ray had never been to visit her before; he hadn't even been to her funeral, so he had no idea as to how to behave at a gravestone. However, the least he was expecting himself to do was freeze at the sight of her name engraved in black Allura letters on the whitewashed stone a few feet away.

The flashes of the past came rushing to his mind with force Ray was unable to stop; the abuse, the rape, the horrible things he did... it all came back and invaded his memory in a way that weakened his legs and brought him to his knees.

It wasn't until that moment that Ray finally realized he hadn't allowed himself to process all the hurt and grief that came with the past. He hadn't allowed himself to dwell enough on those issues; he'd kept them locked away in a safe space and had thrown the key away. However, his arrival back into the city where he'd been born and bred was somehow able to force open that box of unwanted memories, and the hurt, pain, grief, and guilt invaded his mind.

As he knelt by his mother's gravestone, he was being overtaken by all those emotions, and they prompted him to let go of his manliness to the point of tears;

Ray wept.

He cried his eyes out because of his guilt; he was the reason his mom's remains were now lying six feet under the stone that marked her grave, the reason his brother with whom he shared a womb was equally dead. So he mourned the death of his family.

He mourned how they'd met unappealing ends and how it could have been better. He could have made it all better, but he hadn't.

Ray sobbed because, regardless of being a nationally recognized hero, he was such a failure. His father thought so. The brother who'd been born just minutes after him and had shared every childhood event thought so.

And even before he left, his mother had said it to his face. His achievements didn't matter now that he didn't have anyone to share them with in his life. He was just an excuse of a human, living behind the facade of success to cover up for all his mistakes and past shame.

He was pathetic. In his tears, he apologized for all his wrongdoings. He just kept muttering the words' I'm sorry' into the tailored grass covering his mother's grave for what seemed like hours until he had cried to his fill and the dams finally dried up.

Ray felt oddly embarrassed when a box of tissues was handed over to him by an unknown person. He collected it because it was obvious he'd made a mess of his face and gruffly thanked whoever it was who had brought him the thoughtful gift without turning to look at them. He made sure to do justice to his face before turning around.

His heart dropped to the bottom of his stomach when he realized who it was. "What the actual fuck?!" Ray yelled at the top of his voice and struggled to his feet.

The murderous intent radiated off him caused the good Samaritan to take a few steps back.

"I fucking told you I was taking the rest of the day off, and the next thing you thought to do with your miserable life was to follow me? Really?"

Julia could only take a few steps back in caution.

"I thought–"

"You thought you fucking owned my life because I agreed to be partners with a gold-digging, blood-sucking bitch who leeches off the success of others to build her own career?"

Julia looked genuinely hurt when she replied. "You were new in town; I was looking out for you."

"Last I checked, I didn't ask for your goddamn help!"

Ray wasn't annoyed that Julia was following him. Instead, he was livid because, after all, she witnessed him at his lowest, and the same chick reminded him so much of Liz, Ray's crush. How could he have let his guard down so low?

"I also got new Intel information about the latest body found, and it required that we be there as soon as possible. I didn't have your cell, and I wasn't going to see you until tomorrow. When I found you here and at a weak point, I went back to the car and waited. I know what it means to face lows in public places and not want to be seen. I would never intrude in a moment I am not wanted in."

"Get the fuck outta here!" Ray roared with a loudness that made Julia flinch. It wasn't due to anger that he wanted to be as far away from Jules as possible. It was due to the fact he felt rotten that he'd repaid her thoughtfulness with vile words from his mouth.

"Very well." When Julia replied, it was with a cool tone that betrayed nothing of her emotions. "I'll be waiting in the car." With that, she took large strides out of the graveyard.

Ray felt even more rotten.

He wasn't sure in knowing how he should feel at this point. He was guilty, but it wasn't the guilt of the past anymore; the emotion stemmed from what he'd just done to the redhead who was his partner. He couldn't even begin to think of how he was going to tender his apology for displaying such rash reactions to a kind, thoughtful gesture, so Ray decided he wasn't even going to bother with several words.

He took his time to gather himself together before starting toward the direction his partner had gone. It wasn't long before Ray found the patrol corolla parked with its passenger door open. He hesitantly picked his way toward it.

Jules had her eyes closed; her head was tilted upwards and rested on the headrest of the driver's seat. Even though she'd evidently felt his presence, as he wasn't particularly silent, she made no move to open her eyes or even move a muscle.

Ray kept calling her name, but it yielded no results until he finally gave up and rounded the vehicle towards the passenger's corner. The moment he settled into the seat and closed the door, his partner's eyes flung open as if on cue, and her hands swiftly found the vehicle's ignition key and wordlessly turned it on.

In a matter of seconds, they were driving on the road. going where Ray had no idea of where they were going.

The space in the car was caked with tension, and the silence was nerve-wracking. Ray certainly had not felt that uncomfortable since Liz made out with Logan in his presence to prove a point, and even that was very long ago. The urge to apologize was on him more than before, but he suppressed it for some reason and kept staring ahead.

In the very end, he was the one who caved in and said the 's' word.

"I'm sorry."

A few seconds passed before Jules deemed his apology a reply; "Acknowledged." It was a one-worded reply, but a reply all the same.

Then the silence resumed with a vengeance. Ray had to focus on drumming his fingers on his lap to distract his attention from the attractive redhead with an angry blush seated close to him. He was sure she was speeding beyond the regulated speed, but he was too guilty to bring it up.

However, when Jules took a sudden swerve that almost threw him out of the window, Ray was quick to put on his seatbelt, wind up the glass and say a few words of caution;

"Please slow down."

He was barely done talking when the car screeched to a halt due to Jules suddenly stepping on the brake. Ray would have flown out of the windscreen if they did not have a seatbelt.

After the adrenaline rush, not the good kind, had calmed, Ray slowly turned to look at Jules in incredulity. She seemed to be catching her breath as well.

Ray made a mental note never to let her drive him till his duty was over in the city.

"Three things to note before we head in," Jules said as she unhooked her seatbelt, "the last scene of the latest victim was here. We've not visited here prior to now," she pulled out of the car immediately after the second point and flung the door shut.

It took Ray having to walk to his full capacity before he could catch up to her quick, short strides.

"What is the third point to note?" Ray asked as they got to the bouncers, and Jules flashed her badge in front of the man's face.

"The Place is a house of slime and lies. Bring in your A game," Julia whispered as she stepped into the grand establishment of what seemed like a sin.

It was just getting to sunset, yet the strip-slash-BDSM club was already fully into the night's activities. So many things were going on all at once that Ray was almost confused about where to begin. He gave up trying to understand the latter and just marched after Jules' purposeful steps towards God knows where.

She didn't seem to be a stranger to the place as she went through the maze-like passages like a tour guide. Ray could not help but wonder if his partner frequented to satisfy a secret fetish or work a second job.

However, he knew that wasn't the best time to ask, as he had already said things that had kicked his ass off her good book. Ray needed a way to redeem himself, not for a selfish reason, but proper flow and communication in their OP.

Very lost in thought, Ray almost ran into her back before noticing she'd stopped. What looked like a receptionist sized them up as Jules requested to see the manager. The sickly thin girl in lingerie that left little to the imagination asked if they had an appointment with the 'Lead' his partner had asked to see.

"Just mention Eleanor from way back; I'm sure he'll be glad to see us," Julia replied with a hundred-watt beam. The receptionist's gaze lingered lustfully on Ray before she casually pulled up an intercom receiver and pressed an immaculately manicured index on a single button.

Ray was trying to figure out from the short conversation the girl had over the phone and focused on solving the mystery of how Jules knew the manager of a strip club from way back and mentioned an alias.

Ray certainly knew that the conclusion of whatever puzzle he was trying to solve was that Jules had a very wild past.

He was surprised because, in his opinion, she did not look like someone who would indulge in something like that.

Chapter Four.

It wasn't like she didn't have the body for exotic dancing or whatever it was that happened in her wild past; it was just that she looked and seemed a lot like Liz; a straight-A student from kindergarten, privileged and intelligent trust fund baby.

Even now, with her black suit pants, crisp white shirt, and black sports jacket, Jules looked more like a mom to Ray and less like a woman of the wild past.

Ray snapped out of his thoughts when Jules stiffly gestured as they continued down a certain hallway. He could tell she wasn't enjoying her presence in the club and wasn't about to exchange pleasantries with a long-lost lover either.

Jules got to a mirror and stopped. Ray was wondering why the sudden stop when she awkwardly waved in front of it, and the mirror slid open almost immediately. Jules took a couple of deep breaths before walking through an open space of what looked and smelled like a house of orgies rather than some professional office.

The number of naked ladies swarming around the middle-aged man in the room was alarming as it was sickening. Ray looked towards Jules and realized she'd schooled her expression to a small smile. It was so hard to tell what she was feeling at that moment.

"After so long, you finally found your way back to me," the man cooed with a sly smile as he playfully brushed away a few hands that were being overly invasive. "I suppose it is to show me you've scored yourself a man, a hunky one at that. Well, I didn't see that one coming."

"It is nice to see you too after so long, Terry, but I'm here on official business," Jules said as she flashed her badge for Terry to see. The latter let out a rich chuckle before replying,

"I'm sure you're not here to arrest your old man, Eleanor. You and I know that's not possible. I haven't broken any law."

"While that's not the purpose of my visit, it is only a matter of time before your dirty laundry airs or is exposed for all that have eyes to see." Ray noticed that bitterness was beginning to seep into Jules' reply, and maybe that was why she stopped talking.

Ray mentally noted that whatever past it was that Jules shared with this man was one that she regretted.

"For what I'm about to say, privacy would be greatly appreciated, please." Jules looked at all the naked flesh as she talked to drive her point home.

Ray noticed all the naked women in the room seemed to look alike. There were about a dozen of them around him and a dozen more on the different beds and poles that made the most of the room; they were in all shapes and sizes, doing one sinful thing to their own body or experimenting with something new with one another.

However, they all seemed to be wearing ginger-colored wigs, which seemed oddly suspicious to Ray.

"This is my private space, madam; you either say what you're here to say right now or be on your merry way." The light tone Terry was conversing with was gone and in its place was a cold one that held a dangerous threat.

"Very well then, I'm sure you read the news enough to know that your golden girl, Gillian Rivera, has fallen victim to a serial killer. We got word that this was the last place she was seen and that put you on top of the list of our prime suspects–" Jules was interrupted by a sudden order roaring by the aging man.

That was a definite cue to the ladies to begin filing out of the room through a different exit from the one they'd come in.

Terry waited till the last one of them finished before speaking up; "you cannot prove anything." Even though he sounded very sure and determined to give nothing away, shock and fear were evident in his eyes.

"That's the reason why I—we are here. We want to gather facts and prove the truth. If you're cooperative, there will be no need to bring you with us for questioning."

"What do you need?" Terry questioned almost immediately.

"The CCTV footage from Gilligan's day of disappearance will do for now," Jules also replied without missing a beat.

Even though Jules thought she had him, Ray saw Terry's reply coming when he looked deflated almost immediately after the question was answered.

"I'm sorry, Eleanor, but due to our client's privacy policy, we do not keep security cameras in or around The Place, not to mention harvesting their footage. I'm so sorry. I'll be glad to assist if there's anything else I could help with."

Because Ray saw Terry's reply coming, he could also sniff out the lies the older man was spouting. He looked towards Jules to communicate his findings, but it seemed she was already in on the lies as well. She was sporting a deep frown.

"You're the most horrible person I've ever seen, and I don't know why it still amazes me that you keep beating your own record every single time. How can you lie through your teeth in this manner and tell me there are no CCTV cameras in this entire building? Just how?"

It seemed Jules was a little more affected by the lies because she was close to tears by the time she was done talking. Terry could only shrug in mock innocence as though he had no idea what he was saying. Ray walked closer to where Jules stood and suggested they leave. Her head snapped up in disbelief.

"You're not seriously going to leave here without the evidence we came in for, are you? Don't tell me you believe that wretched fellow about the absence of security cameras. That's all a fucking lie!"

Indeed, there was more to that particular lie that greatly affected Jules.

"We can come back when we have proof to counter his claims," Ray whispered to her in such a low tone that it was inaudible to Terry.

"And how do we get those?" Jules asked in her troubled, audible tone, and Ray straightened with a smirk.

"I have my ways." It wasn't a whisper anymore.

After a moment of deliberation, Jules finally decided to trust his plan and nodded. It took minutes for her to regain her composure. They thanked Terry and were soon out of the club before anything unexpected came up.

"You better have a good plan in place to come up with tangible proof. It's almost a week since the death of the last victim, and that can only mean one thing," Jules shared her concern as they walked towards her patrol car.

Ray waited until they were within the confines of the car, with him in the driver's seat, before responding to Jules' concerns;

"Troyer is my secret weapon when it comes to hacking into databases and all of the tech nitty-gritty whenever I'm working on a case. Getting that footage is a piece of biscuit to him. His flight is due to land in about forty-five minutes. Would you like to come with me to pick him up from the airport?"

"I thought you said you could figure out this case with a flashlight and a notepad," Jules taunted in a matter-of-factly tone as she handed him the key to rev the engine.

Ray rolled his eyes and silently drove out of the most uncomfortable place he'd ever been to in a long time.

Julia could see the slight annoyance in Ray's demeanor as she chatted with an excited Troyer. All through the drive back from the airport, his jaw had been ticking like clockwork, and it didn't get better when Julia invited Troyer to stay with her while they figured out a place to stay.

Ray had snapped that he'd already had their accommodation taken care of even before his own arrival into the city.

Now that they were all now settled in the cozy Airbnb Ray had taken residence in, his temper still hadn't improved, and Julia suspected it was due to his jealousy that he was being that way.

She immensely enjoyed Troyer's company, not because of his obvious immediate attraction towards her, but because he was nice overall. He wasn't empathetic about his vulnerability; he smoked weed, hooked her up with a few pills that were sure to empower a good, dreamless night's rest, made good conversations, and didn't mind the flirting.

He was super good at his job, too; he'd already hacked into The Place's database in the course of the drive over and retrieved the files. Each had taken a chunk of the day the victim reported last seen, and all they were currently doing was watching their respective chunk.

While Troyer and Julia made small talk as they went through their respective chunks of the footage, she noticed the alarming increase in Ray's intake of alcohol. At first, she said nothing, but when he'd finished his third bottle of beer and chugged halfway through the fourth in a single gulp, Julia couldn't hold herself anymore. "Slow down, please."

Those were his exact words when she'd been speeding way above the traffic limit, she realized, and they hadn't been effective when he said them, so she added a new sentence that should make up for her shortcomings;

"You won't effectively watch your chunk of footage if you're busy getting drunk."

It was as though Ray had been waiting for her to talk, and he attacked the moment she finished. "And the amount of slutty flirting you've been busy doing is your source of inspiration for effectiveness, hmm?"

Julia is feeling off guard.

"Hey!" Troyer exclaimed in shock, but Ray was too invested in his anger to even care about his friend's surprise.

"Stay the fuck out of this, Troy," Ray bellowed as he stood to his feet.

Julia was already tired of his tantrums. It wasn't even up to twenty-four hours that they'd known each other, and she was getting abused emotionally constantly more times than she could even count.

She had been planning in her mind to sleep over at his place before, but as it currently stood, Julia was already picking up her stuff to head out. She didn't mind that it was way past midnight already.

"You can choke on your beer till dawn, asshole. The bitterness matches your soul anyways."

Chapter Five.

The darkness was eerie, and shadows were thick in the moonless night, yet he could see her. Even in the stark darkness, he was able to make out her figure running away from the house to her car. Something must have happened in the building for her to risk coming out at this point when she knew he was still yet to be caught.

She must have a lot of faith in her service pistol, or her partner had really annoyed her to the point of throwing caution to the wind. He knew her narcissistic partner enough to know what his capabilities were. However, the Carver was too mesmerized to even put much thought into what must have happened in the house.

His most coveted prize had just been within his reach; all he had to do was stretch out his hands, and he could have had her in his arms. The delicate scent of her perfume still lingered in the air even after she drove off. He took his time taking lung full breaths of the scent and held himself from reaching for his member.

Of all his trophies, he knew if he were successful with this one, it would be his most cherished. He'd waited so long to claim this price and was glad his girlfriend had finally given the go-ahead to begin the watch, or he would have started without her consent.

He'd waited this long in the first place because of the unfortunate incident that unexpectedly happened years ago. He'd vowed nothing like that was ever going to happen again. He would make sure to profile this one well and design someone to take the fall for it if everything went south.

He already had the perfect prey in mind.

The torment of seeing several bald women flashing Julia on the night of a full moon wasn't anything she'd bargained for, but that awaited her the minute she closed her eyes and succumbed to her drug-induced sleep. It didn't help that she'd taken pills hoping to get a good night's sleep. It had been as though the pills only sponsored more craziness that saturated her nightmare.

She was back in The Place again, and instead of smoking hot, scantily clad women, the entire club was littered with dead-cold, scantily clad women who sported hysterical laughter and a skin full of gory gashes.

At first, they all had beautiful orange wigs and vibrant makeup. Still, all of a sudden, their wigs disappeared, their colorful faces swiftly began to turn ashen, and their respective bold red lips morphed into chapped, blue ones that sported smiles of mockery.

Of the three faces that stood out for her, two looked a little bit more alive than the rest, but there was nothing left of their torsos but the bloody, hollow remains of their skeletons and the mangled mess of the flesh was torn in a manner so Julia could see through them.

The third, the one closest to Julia, grabbed onto her arm and kept simultaneously muttering the words; 'no' and 'hero.' The walking dead body seemed familiar to her. Still, it wasn't until the body tore open her black lingerie and showed Julia the patterned lacerations slashed deeply into her skin with a scalpel that she finally recognized the body as Gillian's.

The initial smile on Gillian's face morphed into a grim frown as soon as recognition was established, and her beady, lifeless eyes held Julia's pair captive. As she breathed the words that brought dread to settle upon Julia like dew on the grass,

'You're one of us; he's coming for you too.'

Those words had been the climax that jerked Julia awake from the night of horror. They were the same words that haunted her as she hurried through her morning routine and got dressed for work.

It was another early day at work for Julia, as Peter had called her once again to show up early. His delivery sounded less excited than the day before and more solemn, with an added substance of urgency that freaked Julia out.

What made it all the more foreboding was the fact her annoying as-hell partner had texted her an address out of the blue and begged her to get there as soon as possible;

269, brogue way.

Please make your way here ASAP.

It's important.

Ray.

The emphasis was on the word 'please.'

Julia barely touched her breakfast before locking up and rushing into her car. The last words of her nightmare haunted her as she tore through town to get through to the address.

To distract herself from a panic or anxiety attack, Julia put a call through to the number she'd received the text from, but she was sent right to voicemail. She went on to text a response to Ray to inform him she was on her way but didn't get a text back either. As a last resort, she called Peter because she was sure the man would never ignore her.

She wasn't wrong; he picked up on the first ring.

"What is going on, Peter? I'm on the verge of losing my mind here." Julia yelled into the receiver the moment the call connected. It wasn't until she was done talking that she heard the noises in the background and put two and two together to conclude her boss wasn't in the office that Wednesday morning.

She anxiously waited for his response.

"Why are you not here yet? I think Ray said he texted you the address of where you're supposed to be."

Julia's nervousness skyrocketed when she heard what Peter had to say.

"I'm almost there. Please tell me I'll be coming to follow up on a lead and not to check out a body." The line went dead immediately, and it was all the validation Julia needed to confirm that another body had been discovered.

Her heart sank a little further down her chest.

Once again, they wasted precious time and failed, even though the FBI sent a special agent to run the OP. The killer had once again outsmarted them and taken yet another life.

Little did she know she was going to get the shock of her life, and it wasn't the cleared-out perimeter or the several 'do not cross' and 'crime scene' tapes that crisscrossed everywhere as she reached, pulled up her car to a stop and clambered out.

As she drew closer to where the unmistakable form of her partner and her boss stood amongst a crowd of photographers and pathologists, she was surprised to see not one but two body bags. The surprise didn't end there.

On arrival at the scene, Julia stiffened at the sight of the faces in both body bags. She clasped her hands on her mouth in shock and took hurried steps backward that would have made her trip over herself if Ray wasn't around to pull her to him with a force that made her helplessly collide against his body.

Julia would have winced in pain or embarrassment if she wasn't currently going through a mental meltdown.

She wanted to think this was just another nightmare, but Julia knew better than denial at this point. Yet, she was still in disbelief as to how possible what she'd witnessed could be true.

What were the odds? What were the fucking odds they would be discovering two new bodies in the heart of the city three days, just three days after pulling another one out of a river?

What were the odds she'd turned into some extreme psychic and predicted the next two victims and possibly the exact way they would meet their gruesome ends?

What really were the odds?

"Are you okay, Jules?" It wasn't until she heard Peter's soothing tone that Julia realized she had involuntarily called unwanted attention toward herself.

"I saw those faces in my dreams last night. They were being gutted like a fish very horribly." Julia came out clean without mincing words and burst into tears almost immediately.

Peter was surprised by her proclamation and outburst, but he understood the case so far had been seriously taking a toll on her mental health of late, and she really did need an outlet. His arms wrapping around her, he held onto her in his normal way of showing that fatherly care Julia had come to miss.

He waited till she had gone from the heavy, body-wracking sobs to just whimpers and occasional hiccups before letting her go.

Low key, Peter also suspected she'd probably know one or both of the bodies personally and was probably mourning them, and he was fine with that too. He made sure to leave her in the care of Ray before going back to the crime scene proper to coordinate the happenings there and pack up the body before the press came poking noses into the entire affair and driving at ridiculous headlines.

Ray and Jules sat side by side in awkward silence as the latter tried to catch her breath and put herself together. She was embarrassed that Ray and everyone else had to witness her breakdown in such a humiliating manner. Still, she focused on cleaning up the mess she made on her face instead of facing the embarrassment she'd caused herself.

The silence lasted a few more moments before Ray broke it with a ludicrous statement;

"He sure doesn't look like your sugar daddy with all those closeness y'all just displayed right there."

Jules would have flared up immediately. He hadn't even cared about her breakdown in the least, but she was too exhausted to do so. She let out a sigh that came out as a shaky breath and pulled out what seemed like a medallion from the black turtleneck she was sporting that morning.

"Peter lost the love of his wife and her twin babies in a fire accident just two years after his twins were born. He has distracted himself in work ever since, and I fear that he still hasn't forgiven himself enough to move on." She opened up what turned out to be a picture locket and showed it to Ray. It had a picture of the young sheriff and his wife heavily pregnant.

"So you're his wife's sister helping him cope with the PTSD, I see." Again, Ray's assumption span amazed Julia, but she had already begun her horrible story, so she might as well finish it.

"My mom suffered a hit-and-run case from her high-school crush, and she didn't want a result of it, aka me, so she dumped me at birth with her irresponsible brother a few years younger and took off. I never got to understand or know who she was, and even though her brother took me in, he barely cared for me. I was malnourished all my childhood, and I survived on food aid from kind people.

"My name wasn't in the system as my mother had me at home and ran off almost immediately. Her brother didn't bother to make me a legal child either, and it was in the slums where nobody really cared about another, so I suffered. I thought that when Terry suddenly had a change of heart and began feeding me, that was the end of my travels. I couldn't have been more wrong.

"He snatched away my cherry at twelve and continued to abuse me till I was old enough to be pimped to his friends and, ultimately, the makers and shakers of the city. I tried, severally, to run away over the years, but Terry kept finding me, and every time he did, he'd punish me in a more dire way than the last time. In the long run, I stopped trying.

"The Place was built on my sweat and my blood. All the long-standing patrons of that blasted club knew Eleanor: the broken beauty, and took out every last one of their sick fantasies on her..."

Julia finally trailed off, her eyes glossy with tears. She spent the next few seconds catching her breath and blinking away the tears. She resumed with a calmer voice,

"I was sterilized against my will to avoid the same mistake my mother made when she conceived me. I spent eleven years, five at The Place, being raped continuously by several men. I lived my life on drugs and substances to escape reality and prayed every night for a miracle to happen, and when it seemed like it was all for naught, the miracle came in the form of Peter.

"He raided The Place and took all the strippers and sex workers into custody. I was the only one he didn't release because I begged to remain in jail. After he heard every ordeal I had been through, he decided to bargain for my freedom with Terry, took me in, saw me through the police academy, and the rest is history.

"Peter gave me this pendant when I moved out to a place of my own. In case Terry ever comes to kidnap me again, it has a tracking chip embedded in it that activates when I press down on the locket. He had it made as an SOS signal to him and promised to come calling the moment I pressed on it. Even though I haven't ever pressed on it, it has never left me. I cherish it as a daughter would a gift from her father."

It was silent after Julia finally finished her horrific story. Aside from the sirens, clicks of several cameras, and the voices of the men working on the crime scene, all of which seemed distant, the man seated beside her at the back of the sheriff's pickup was awfully silent.

She turned towards him to see that his eyes widened to his dismay; it seemed Ray was still processing all the information she'd just told him.

Her attention was distracted by a chime that came from the phone in her jeans pocket. She pulled it out to read a text that came from Peter himself;

We have to meet back at the department, grab your partner, and head on ahead.

Chapter Six.

"Peter wants us back at the department as soon as possible. We need to head out now," Jules suddenly announced and jumped to her feet as if she hadn't just told Ray the most heart-breaking story he'd ever heard.

It was hard to believe that the woman, who was now marching towards her patrol van with such agility and poise, had been through so much and yet still stood strong.

It was hard to believe some people had it worse than him in the course of their childhood.

When Jules drove her patrol car close to him, he silently got into the passenger seat and closed the door. She drove moderately this time, but even if she'd exceeded the speed limit to the max, Ray still wouldn't have been able to mutter a word.

He was still processing the entire thing, trying to make sense of how even after having such a terrible past, Jules still lived like a normal being and had a positive outlook on life. He wondered how she'd managed to make it through those dark years of her life and why Jules still had kept going in her dark tunnel for over two decades, even when there was no light in sight.

Ray wondered how she could live through her childhood with nothing to hope for or look forward to in life.

It was all tragic; everything Jules had gone through to get to where she was now. He now understood why she'd thrown tantrums at the beginning of their introduction, why she'd understood him at his point of weakness, and why she looked towards the older man with such adoration and love.

She wasn't a privileged trust fund baby; she'd been through thick and thin and had worked her way up legitimately in her career. Jules deserved a cape, and he was wrong to pass the wrong kinds of judgment upon her from the onset until now.

She'd earned Ray's respect. "I'm sorry," he whispered loud enough for her to hear, and Jules nodded promptly.

"Acknowledged." Ray looked at her strangely, and she shrugged even though she didn't match his gaze with hers. "Even though I try, I realize I cannot hold grudges. Especially when the offender is remorseful and grovels for forgiveness with sparse words."

A hint of a smile was on her face as she pulled into the driveway of the department. Ray realized it was an attempt at humor, smiling genuinely for the first time in a while.

"Thank you," he said sincerely.

"You're welcome. Now that we've started on the right foot and are on the right page, let's focus all our energy on catching this criminal, yeah?"

Ray nodded in agreement. He was tired of fighting too.

"I gathered from Martha, the only victim that'd managed to escape this killer; she says he calls himself the Carver," Douglas, Jules' previous partner, said with an air of importance.

Ray almost rolled his eyes.

"What else were you able to gather from the witness?" He asked the nerdy-looking officer, and seemingly all the confidence the man had gathered to say the first sentence fled immediately.

"I... uh. It's all she was ready to tell me at the first interview with her. I couldn't get her to agree to any further questioning before being killed." Douglas stuttered his reply, and there was a collective sigh.

The four of them, Ray, Jules, McCain, and Douglas, were all in the sheriff's office trying to connect all the dots and arrest suspects at least. There have been no arrests since the first body washed up on shore five weeks ago, and the press began to publish things that couldn't be farther from the truth. They needed to work together to catch the criminal before another set of bodies were discovered, maybe by children and students.

"So far, we can tell that his targets are women of questionable livelihoods. We've recovered eight bodies, all of which belong to exotic dancers, nudists, and sex workers."

Peter penned down Jules' observation on a sticker note and placed it on the part of the whiteboard that had the victim's question mark.

"From my conversation with the pathologist who profiled the last bodies, there were traces of drugs that worked as relaxation when a dentist preps his client for teeth removal. All their vital organs are also always missing. Our guy may be in the medical industry, side hustling as an organ trafficker, which could also explain his target market, as he knows not many people care about the night's women besides their patrons. It would be easy for a few sluts to disappear without raising more than eyebrows."

McCain looked impressed by Ray's contributions; he quickly scribbled the words' medical practitioner' on the space questioning the suspect.

"Excellent observations," Jules piped up. "If the guy is killing multiple victims solely to sell organs, why shave off their hair and keep them as trophies?"

"Maybe he's selling those too, Jules?" McCain quickly answered the question, and then he turned towards Ray. "What do you think?"

"I wouldn't think so, Peter. He is definitely smarter than leaving a trail that'll lead directly to him. The sick dude probably has each shaven hair framed and hanging in his room."

Ray was also about discrediting McCain's contribution before a tiny detail they have been leaving out for a while.

"Don't women sell their hair to be made into wigs?" Douglas beat him to speak this time. "What if he has a discreet way he could sell them off anonymously?"

"I don't think so, Doug. There isn't such a great market for orange wigs. I would know because I've tried shaving off my hair for sale before."

"You what, Jules?" McCain asked in shock.

"Don't worry about it, Pete; it was such a long time ago."

"The last time we visited The Place, Jules. Did you spot anything unusual in Terry's private lounge?" Ray butted in with a tone of urgency.

"All the women being redheads? That's no biggie; Terry has a thing for redheads–"

"What if those were wigs and clip-ins, instead? What if Terry was buying these ladies' wigs from the killer?" Once again, someone beat Ray to say what was just on the tip of his tongue.

It was the sheriff this time.

"Bingo." Even though Ray was displeased by how he was consistently being interrupted, he was glad he wasn't among dunderheads who couldn't think for themselves.

Jules' eyes widened a fraction.

"What if Terry is the killer?" She whispered incredulously and clapped her hand over her mouth almost immediately as though she'd just uttered a taboo.

McCain whirled around and added Terry's name to the suspect tab and three points to the void space with the header 'line of action';

● Raid The Place.

● Impound all redhead wigs on sight to be tested for DNA matches with victims.

● Bring Terry in for questioning.

"These courses of action will be effective immediately." McCain took charge immediately. "Ray, please call in your tech guy. We could use his help to check out recent transactions of Terry's offshore accounts, social media chats, and everything we can get. If Terry is our guy, we need to be two steps ahead of him even before making an arrest."

Ray nodded in acknowledgment and pulled out his phone to call Troyer. He felt bad that his friend's first day after being jet lagged was going to go from being spent in solitude to working under pressure, but there was no other choice. That was the reason he was there in the first place.

However, Ray soon realized he was being sent straight to Troyer's voicemail. He immediately suspected his tech druggy was probably high on one form of substance or another. He would have to get back to his apartment to shake him to his senses.

McCain readily agreed to Ray's to get to his apartment.

"That's fine; as soon as you get across to him and begin work, let me know. Douglas, Jules, and I will pick up a few boys and flesh out The Place. We'll let you know how it goes. Keep in touch."

The urgency in the air made it impossible to get any other observation to the notice of his other partners, but it was fine. They were on to a good start already, and he was going to tell Troyer to look at the medical practitioners in the immediate areas of finding the recent bodies.

Chapter Seven.

Ray realized he had no means to get to his apartment after Jules and her boss had rushed out of the department with a few vehicles and sirens blaring. He walked to the side of the street where he could easily hitch a ride.

Ray stayed by the roadside for a while and waved several taxis down before a driver finally decided to stop. He took his time to tell the driver the address and ensure he knew where he was heading before entering the vehicle and settling down.

It wasn't until after the driver began the journey, as he watched the busy streets of the city wheeze by, that Ray finally attended to the thousand and one questions that kept running across his mind.

He began thinking about the ongoing case and how, even though it seemed like they were finally getting headway, something somewhere was wrong. Ray tried to suppress his instincts, but he just knew Terry wasn't the killer, and they would be making a humongous mistake if they arrested Terry and relaxed.

However, time was no longer on his side to prove that. Ray needed Troyer's opinion on all of it now more than ever.

"We have to crack this case before another dead body shows up," he muttered as he turned on his phone and tried to call his hacker friend Troyer.

He wondered why he hadn't heard a word from Troyer since he left the house about eight hours ago. That was very unlike him, even in his high state. Ray grew more anxious when his call connected straight to voicemail for the umpteenth time that afternoon.

"Hello there, it's a regret that Troyer is currently unreachable at the moment, but it's just for a few minutes, I promise. Kindly call back, or leave a message if it's urgent. Tiddies!" It was the recorded message that answered the call in Troyer's stead.

He requested "driver step on the gas" while he distracted his mind by thinking about the clues behind which the team had omitted. He thought about the clues they had found, the ones they didn't read much meaning into, which would have created a lead in the case.

He thought about how the potential suspects would have paved more ways to cracking the criminal case, who the killer really was, how to lure the killer out of his hiding place, and realizing how much time they had left before another dead body showed up.

Ray knew he might have the most to lose in this case, as his impeccable reputation was on the verge of being stained should another body emerge without cracking the case. Not only would Logan laugh at him, but Liz would also be happy to boast and shame Melissa for believing in him.

"Something has to happen soon, and this has to be quick," He muttered.

The driver instantly thwarted his thought process, who had just notified him that he had gotten to his destination. Ray looked out of his window and realized that he'd indeed gotten to his abode. However, for some reason, his initial enthusiasm to get to the apartment had waned, and in its place was this awful foreboding feeling and hesitance he could not place.

"Hey, Sir, you've just arrived at your destination," the driver repeated with a calm tone, and Ray snapped from his sentiments, pulled out his wallet to retrieve some money, paid the driver with an extra tip, and thanked him for his patience.

"Have yourself a lovely day," Ray added with a smile as he made his way to get out of the car.

The driver started the car and zoomed off as soon as he did; Ray heaved a sigh of exhaustion and waited for a few hesitant seconds before he began making his way toward the steps of his block. He got to the entrance of his apartment sooner than later, only to find out that his door was ajar.

Ray noticed the feeling of exhaustion fled, and his senses heightened to a peak. Out of suspicion, he brought out his service pistol and slowly opened the door without making a noise. He then began tiptoeing across his sitting room and looking around to see if anyone was in his house. But, to his greatest surprise, Troyer wasn't in.

Even though there had been no signs of struggle or scuffle, Ray was now very alarmed. He began searching his apartment, piece by piece, with his service pistol firmly in his grasp, ready to be fired, from the sitting room to the three bedrooms, their closets, and even their bathrooms. Yet he found nothing.

Everything was intact, not even a sign of Troyer's normal shenanigans.

He went to his room again to be sure he wasn't currently getting pranked by his friend. He even searched through his stuff and found nothing out of place.

He burst open the backdoor and then began to check around to see any possibility of anyone sniffing around the environment. Still, he found nothing.

Right there and then, Ray began doubting Troyer's safety. But still, he managed to check through his room until he heard a loud thud coming from his entrance. He immediately ran towards the noise to see what was going on. When he got to the door linking to the backyard, he slowed down and began to tiptoe.

He slowly opened the door and pointed out his service pistol, and he rushed outside to see what was there, but he found nothing. He finally gave up, sighed, and began to make his way back to his room. He wanted to get a drink from the refrigerator when his eyes mistakenly fell on a box on his kitchen counter.

All of Ray's calmed guard rose back up, and he drew closer. He noticed a note attached to the tip of the box. He then looked around to see if anybody had come in to drop a box of whatever it contained. He reached for the note on top of the box, and the writing he saw on the piece of paper could only be none other than Troyer's scratchy handwriting.

Relief is written over his face as he plucked the note from the travel box.

*** "Hey Bud,

I'm sorry I had to leave. Liz called when something came up at the headquarters that needed my expertise and told me she was coming to town to help with the case.

As much as I hate to leave, I'm glad you all will spend time together. Who knows? You may finally get what you deserve.

PS: Liz was the one who sent the box of clothes, and I took some out for me because they just looked good on me.

Love, Troyer"

"Oh my God! Liz is coming to Manhattan. That is great news! I will be able to get near her finally."

Ray did not heed or warn of the sirens blaring his head. As he read through the note, or how it was odd for Liz to send Troyer over to him when she liked direct dealings, and then why Troyer had to write a note instead of sending in a text or how it was never like Troyer to agree that Liz was good for him or finish his sentence with 'love, Troyer.' All that mattered the most to him was Liz was coming into town.

He said it as his face beamed with joy as he read through the piece of paper, then slammed the refrigerator without even minding the fact that he had injured himself. After reading the note on the box, he hurriedly dropped the gun and unzipped the box open. He ran through the clothes one piece after the other until he unfolded the last one. While spreading out the last one for inspection, an item fell, and Ray, out of a knee-jerk reaction, caught it in mid-air.

It was a scalpel.

In that moment of discovery, Ray dropped the scalpel and then started to get a gut feeling of uneasiness. He began wondering how the scalpel got there and who would even put it there. He made up his mind, and he was going to ask Liz when she arrived. While thinking all that through, he decided to inform Troyer, his best friend. He tried putting a call through to Troyer, but the number was not going through.

Maybe it was because he was on a flight, he thought. He decided to put a call through to Liz instead, and while her phone rang, it didn't connect until he got the voicemail.

"Liz, please pick up the call, would you?" He tried again, but the number still wouldn't connect. He went to voicemail.

It was unlike Liz because she never left her calls unanswered, especially when it was business. Ray wondered what on earth was going on.

He was still busy thinking things through when his phone chimed. It was a text from Liz.

"Hey Ray,

Good evening from this end. I just touched down, so I can't talk now. I'm on the way from the airport. I didn't want to bother you to come to pick me up; I'll find my way over to yours.

I'm guessing you just got the delivery I sent to you; the box of clothes. I want you to check them out and send some pictures of you in them, so I can decide which one I want you to wear tonight.

I also want you to wait till I get there before laying your hands on any official duties; that's an order. You can continue with work after showing me around and having dinner at a nice restaurant; I can't wait to see you again.

See you soon, Liz."

Ray sighed as he read through the message and was grinning from ear to ear by the time he finished going through it. He sent a call to Melissa and tried to confirm with her if it was true that Liz was leaving all the headquarters duties to come all the way down to Manhattan and have dinner with an agent that was no secret to anyone that she hated. But to no avail; Melissa didn't answer either.

Ray waited for years to have a chance with Liz, and it seemed like he would have the opportunity to show her once and for all. However, Ray began to wonder about what having Liz in his house and around him would feel like, having known that Liz was his boss and his crush. His emotions were going in a seesaw pattern, with dopamine on one end and fear on the other.

He started to think about his firsts with his long-term crush as he brought down the box from the counter and wheeled it towards his bedroom, his initial foreboding feeling buried deep beneath all the new, flowery ones.

He's been trying to check in on his team or update them about the recent changes, but Ray was frustrated that nobody would answer their phones. He spent some time trying on the outfits and sending pictures to Liz for her to make the best choice in his attire for the evening.

Little did Ray know that Liz was setting him up for the biggest failure of his life, and he was busy digging his own shallow grave.

Chapter Eight.

A deadly nightmare was what Julia had jerked awake from that morning. That was already the big tell that the day wouldn't be good. She immediately reached for her phone to dial a certain number, but she didn't get that far. A text from Peter was already waiting for her;

We got the Carver, Jules. It's not Terry.

Julia felt satisfied they had caught the killer, but dread settled like goosebumps on her skin because it wasn't Terry. It was still a few minutes to five, but she finished her routine in five minutes and dashed out of her apartment in less time. She blasted full speed towards the station while trying to connect with Peter, but for some reason, he would not pick up her calls.

She pulled into the driveway to see why Peter would not even hear his phone ring. Vehicles of at least twenty media houses are parked haphazardly in the driveway. Several bright flashes and equally several people clamoring to be let into the station while Peter was outside with an entire battalion trying to keep a stampede from happening. Julia knew there was no way to get into the station without breaking a bone unless she went through the back and ran the risk of being followed.

In the end, she decided to run the risk of the latter. She came down from the vehicle and went through the back. Luckily, everyone had been too agitated to go through the front that they hadn't noticed her slip by them.

She was in the office in no time and retraced her path back to the front door, where Peter stood.

The older man left instructions with the police officers and rushed towards her when he noticed her presence. He hugged her briefly and began to drag her towards his office without a word. He ensured to secure the latches and locks, close his windows and draw the blinds before even answering her salutation.

"I got your text, Peter; what on earth is going on?" Julia asked, worried as Peter rounded his desk to access the safe behind his swivel chair.

"Well, I thought the text was self-explanatory," Peter replied as he worked on the lock combination of the safe.

"Well, you only told me it's not Terry; you didn't say who it was? Why is Ray not here, by the way? I had a terrible dream about him last night, and he still isn't picking up my calls."

While Julia was ranting, Peter had fished out his desired document from the vault and stretched it towards Jules without a word. Jules collected it in puzzlement and slowly put her hands inside to bring out what it contained.

"You might want to sit down and take a deep breath before doing that," Peter warned, but it was already too late. Her heart stopped for a full second when she saw what the envelopes revealed.

The room suddenly began to spin out of focus.

"What?" She found herself whispering in disbelief. She didn't even realize Peter was holding her to himself until he spoke from behind her.

"I'm going to need you to stay calm."

"It's not just possible, Pete. How can you believe something as frivolous as this when you know Photoshop exists?"

"He isn't who you think he is, Jules. He fooled all of us–"

"No, that's just not possible–"

"He has a criminal record, Jules."

"So do I, Pete."

"He went to Juve for forcing himself on his mother twice, Jules."

Jules had already opened her mouth to say something in defense before her brain processed what Peter had just said.

"What?" Is what all she could say.

"Yes. I checked his records after getting this anonymously delivered to my residence. We burst into his apartment early this morning and retrieved his tortured boss from his basement. The woman called Liz, in her hysteria, said he'd tried to kill her the night before. Before being rushed to the hospital, she also attested that he'd just gotten back from a six-week leave. We retrieved so much incriminating evidence, including several scalpels, body bags, clothes that match the pictures you saw, a Polaroid camera, and a video recording of him carving through our latest victims. We've sent them all out for testing, but it's too early to get back reports.

It's obvious someone had tipped the press and leaked the news. We have nothing to say to the press or the public, which is where I'll need you to come in. He's nothing but a suspect, for now, but if you can get him to admit his crime, then we may be able to have something to say."

Julia was still too dumbfounded to comprehend what Peter was saying.

The same man she'd partnered with to find the killer was indeed the killer, and Peter wanted her to face the same man she was beginning to consider a friend and press him to admit he'd killed so many ladies in a span he was supposed to go off work and unwind.

It all did not add up. At all.

She listened to her boss as he continued to state more facts that further nailed Ray to the cross, but there was nothing she could do about it. Everything she'd seen and heard was tangible proof, yet she still could not believe it was all true.

In the end, she begged Peter to give her time to process, to deal with everything;

"Let me clear my head and collect myself," She begged, "I want to bring in my all to finish this."

Peter conceded and asked her to take her time.

Indeed, Julia took her time. It wasn't until the evening that she finally gathered enough mental capacity to face the alleged criminal. By then, all the evidence was clear that they'd found their killer.

Ray was not ready to explain how he found his boss in the basement of his Airbnb apartment, a basement he didn't know existed until that morning. Even if he had wanted to, he wasn't sure the dozen of armed and stern-looking men that arrested him would be willing to listen to his explanations.

Not after a terrified Liz had told them he'd tried to kill her the night before.

That was why he had silently followed all the orders they'd barked at him without breathing a word.

Now that he looked at the tough-looking redhead who had come to interrogate him, how she looked ready and skillful to snap his neck in two if he as much as moved a muscle, he still wasn't sure that she would believe his side of the story.

How could he explain to this woman, his partner, that he had no prior knowledge of the added space beneath his apartment up until that morning? How does Ray tell this woman who looked like she wanted to stab him with her stares? He was expecting Liz's arrival; he hadn't seen her, either alive or semi-dead, until armed men burst in and brought her out of his kitchen; his guess was as good as hers about the killer.

How could Ray explain that his fingerprints detected all over the parts of Liz's body was something that even left him puzzled? How could he convince Jules this was a complete setup? The last person he'd ever hurt was his boss and crush. How would his interrogator believe he couldn't hurt a rat in cold blood, let alone not talk about people he didn't know from Adam?

There were many things he couldn't even begin to comprehend, like how he didn't bother to explore his own apartment and how whoever it was that had gathered a lot of incriminating evidence against him had been able to do all of it without his knowledge or even suspicion. Had he lowered his guard to a level that he was set up to such perfection, or was he just plain stupid?

"I didn't do it, Jules." was all he could manage to say in a low tone.

Julia did not bother with words; she only pulled out a brown envelope from the file she'd come along with, brought a single Polaroid out of the several others Peter had received that morning from an anonymous source, and pushed it towards him.

Ray hesitantly picked up the image for scrutiny after his fruitless attempt at getting more information about the image from the woman who looked at him with so much detachment that he would have confused her for a stranger if he hadn't known better.

There was no doubt that a high-quality camera had taken the picture. Hence, regardless of the blurry background and overall dark environment, the image was clear enough for Ray to see himself handling a glistening scalpel in his right hand and standing directly above what seemed like a woman struggling against the ropes holding her firmly to a chair.

In one of the clothes that'd been delivered to his doorstep just the night before.

The man, who could not recollect himself doing these things, could not contain his shock.

"I didn't do it!" He screamed in a high-pitched tone and tried to shield his eyes from the horror unfolding as Jules supplied more graphic images and ultimately began to play a video. Alas, his hands behind him with a handcuff firmly binding him.

Ray had no choice but to watch a video of evidence that he killed the latest victim, sliced through their torso, and bagged up their organs.

Ray watched in horror as he sliced the dead bodies into a mangled mess. Then after the entire exercise, he moved towards a part of the room that seemed darker than the rest and performed a peculiar dance before walking over to the camera to end the video.

Then as though the blank screen of the device signified the end of the video was the cue for all the missing pieces of the puzzle to materialize and click into place finally, Ray finally realized what was going on.

However, it wasn't a realization that brought about a pleasant feeling; instead, his blood ran cold.

"Jules, you've got to believe me; that wasn't me." His tone was even more urgent this time, but Jules only looked on in indifference.

"Someone set me up. I promise you. If it's the person I think it is, I would be paying for a crime I didn't commit once again, and even that will not stop him from killing more people."

Jules looked straight into his eyes for a few seconds and stood to her feet.

"You're going to pay for everything you did, whether you admit it or not," were the only words she uttered before she began walking out of the room.

"I'm begging you, Jules. Leave your SOS on tonight. If he came for Liz, I think he's no longer sticking to the status quo." She didn't seem interested in anything he had to say; Jules was gone even before he finished talking.

Chapter Nine.

The drive away from the department was a reflective one. Julia had no idea what to believe anymore, so she decided to take a drive to clear her head. She started driving in circles because she didn't know where to drive, but when Julia ended up right in front of the bar, she decided to have a couple of drinks to calm her nerves and possibly help her think straight.

Her drink confirmed that her processing method had failed woefully because her mind couldn't stop flip-flopping to Ray's guilt. As her finger glides around the rim of the glass, she grabs the glass to take another drink and sets the glass down on the bar, and mutters, "I don't get it!"

Peter had organized a press conference after the evidence began to troop in; none of them favored Ray. He's the prime suspect in the entire saga and would be prosecuted by the jury as soon as possible.

Her interrogating him was just some form of formality. After what happened in that room and how Ray responded to the videos he'd watched, Julia could not make sense of anything anymore.

"It all doesn't just add up," she said aloud to herself and took a swig of her drink. "Who would have thought Ray was the one behind the killings? How is that even possible?"

Something in her was against everything happening, even though every piece of evidence pointed toward Ray's guilt. Her instincts still wanted to believe Ray was taking the fall somehow.

But why? What would anyone stand to gain by setting him up? Who even knew him enough to do that? The statements in his records showed that he fled and went into exile after killing his brother, which was fifteen years ago. Even Peter hadn't remembered him when he returned, so who held a grudge long enough to wait for him to come back?

Her thought process is thwarted suddenly by a stranger tapping at the flat platform in front of her. Julia looked up to see an attractive-looking woman in her late thirties.

"Hello, Miss, my husband and I have been watching you, and we felt you were a little bit lonely. If you don't mind, I'd like you to come to sit at our table and have some fun time with us," were the words that came out of the middle-aged woman. Julia looked at the table towards the corner of the bar room and saw a man seated with his back turned to her; suddenly, her gaze returned to the focused one of the attractive ladies.

"I'm so sorry, but I need my space, so, if you don't mind, kindly excuse me; l am sorta in the middle of something," Julia blurted without thinking.

"Something like what?" the blonde woman questioned. Julia's brow shot up in suspicion, but she said nothing in response.

The lady's smile swiftly began to morph into a fearsome sick grimace, but she still did not budge from her position.

"Alright. I'm sorry. My name is Karen, and my man is over there; his name is Ryan. He would be very pleased to meet you if you would just–"

"Karen or whatever your name is," Julia interrupted rudely. "l thought l just told you that I'm in the middle of something and I need my space. I'm trying to figure something out, and you come here, all willy-nilly, and you're telling me that your name is Karen; how does that help me?"

"Relax, babe, chill. I'm just trying to be a reliable, good citizen here. We saw you were in distress, and we decided to help you recover from whatever you are suffering from," Karen blurted out, her sickly smile now looking more like a sneer.

Julia decided she'd had enough.

"Karen, please. I don't need your help, and please, I wouldn't mind if you stayed away from my personal space. Thank you very much for poke-nosing into my business, wasting my time, and distorting my thinking process. Please leave my presence this minute, or I will call the cops." Julia spoke in a calm tone that belied all her anguish.

"Very well then, see you later in the night," Karen said in a hushed tone and made her way towards her previous seat and whispered something in the man's ear, and they made for the door until Julia called.

"Psst! Hey! You left your purse on the table."

"Ohh! Thank you very much for the reminder." Karen said as she made for her purse and left. Karen almost made it to the door, then she made a U-turn towards Julia, gave a mischievous grin, and said in a hushed tone, "See you around."

When Julia saw that, she felt an uneasiness shiver down her spine. Feelings of wonderment, perplexity, and fear pounced on her as she watched Karen gaze at her through the glass she was sitting close to, which wasn't far from Karen's car.

The words of Ray came back to Julia as she tried to shove all the emotions aside and just concentrated on her drink;

'I'm begging you, Jules. Leave your SOS on tonight. If he came for Liz, I think he's no longer sticking to the status quo.'

Julia looked out the window once more and saw that the creepy couple was gone; her hand found its way to her locket. She discreetly caressed it and decided, last minute, against pressing on it for the tracking chip to be activated. It was all it took to suppress the shivers of uneasiness that kept coursing through her body.

It didn't take long before Julia downed her sip of beer and ordered another. As she wandered through Memory Lane; How she had met Ray three days ago, How they always had disagreements back to back, how they both had to put up with each other in the line of their duties, how Ray wept profusely on his mother's graveyard and it goes on and on.

Even though three days was too short to finish an analysis of someone's character, Julia could not help but think that she knew Ray to a level. Or was Ray doing that on purpose to gain Julia's trust? What does he think to gain from all of these? Was all the weeping staged to gain her trust and make him seem like a normal human? Why would Ray even do that in the first place? Was he innocent as he claimed to be?

Sitting at the bar rubbing her forehead, Julia started feeling weird, but she played it off by having a stressful day. Julia kept racking her brain as hard as possible on the questions running through her mind, but she couldn't provide the answers. She could only sigh as her head was spinning.

"Ma'am, are you ok?" Julia looked at the bartender, nodded, and waved her hand to him, " Yeah, I'm fine. Drive carefully, and please come back soon, said the barkeep.

"Thank you for your service to humanity." She said as she chuckled nervously. She started to make her way to the exit through the dimly lit and smokey-hazed bar. Once she left the door, her legs began feeling heavier and heavier.

Julia made it to her car when she began to feel nauseous and dizzy. She looked around uneasily, hurriedly entered her car, and turned on the ignition.

Julia knew she wasn't drunk, but she felt like she was about to be sick and someone was watching her; It took her back to her days in Terry's prison when men watched her lustfully, with her raw marks and scars. She was feeling the same way she had felt then.

"Thank the Heavens; my house is just a few blocks away." She muttered to herself as she accelerated her speed. Finally, she made it through her garage, but her legs began to wobble.

The earlier conversation with that creepy lady flashed in her mind as she wobbled towards her door and fumbled with the keys. The woman said something striking that Julia hadn't paid any mind to until the surroundings began to blur out of concentration;

'Very well then, see you later in the night.'

Julia felt a drug coursing through her body without mincing words.

With the last of her strength, she felt for her locket and pressed on it, hoping that Peter had been serious about barraging down with all of Hell's fury the minute she called for it.

Julia Wakened to a pounding headache, parched throat, and overall darkness. If that didn't give away the fact that she had been abducted, the feeling of her wrist and ankles being tied to a chair and her naked butt feeling the coldness of the metal chair was a major validation.

She rolled her head around to feel for her necklace and realized it wasn't there anymore. Her heart hammered to a stop. If the tracker had been taken away before they brought Julia, the hope Peter would come looking for her would have just slimmed down a little more.

Julia was on her own on this one; it was up to her to survive the night or perish. She still did not know why the nice, concerned citizens had swiftly turned villains and were now seeming like they wanted to eat her for dinner.

With her eyes wide open, Julia could sense she was not the only one in the room. Even in thick darkness, one could tell a man and a woman figure in the room. They spoke to themselves in a hushed tone.

"She's awake!"

That was all she heard until there was an outburst of light. The studio-intensity lights momentarily blinded Julia. Still, when her eyes finally got used to the brightness, her face read nothing but surprise, shock, and maybe disappointment when she saw Karen and then...

Ray!

Her jaw dropped to the ground.

Gone was the sincerity and genuineness that begged her to believe him hours ago, and in its place was a cold, primal essence akin to that of a National Geographic predator stalking its prey.

"Surprise!" Karen chimed like a Christmas jingle while Ray looked at her with a self-satisfied smirk plastered.

"So it's been you all along!" Julia found herself yelling. "All those acts were fake? You really are the one who killed–"

"Well, I think there's been a big misunderstanding here," Karen interrupted Julia's surprise outburst with a sickly sweet smile in place. "We don't normally do this, but you're a special one, so say hello to Ray's twin brother, Ryan!"

Just when Julia thought nothing more could shock her,

Boom!

She tried, severally, but failed to come up with anything to think of, not to talk or say.

Was this another nightmare? It had to be that when she'd fallen unconscious on her front porch, her twisted mind had brought her to this warped plane in Lala land.

"While she tries to process all this, kindly sterilize the clipper, baby?" Ray's twin pulled the woman, who was no doubt older than he was close, and kissed her passionately.

When the awfully disgusting make-out session was over, Karen giggled like a high school girl and walked out of Julia's line of sight.

"I've waited this long to have you, Julia. I will cherish every second of this night for as long as I live."

Julia, who was still finding it hard to believe she wasn't currently in the presence of her partner, was too stunned to shiver due to the deadly threat he'd doled out with such eloquence.

"You're supposed to be dead," She stuttered aloud. "This is just not possible."

"I'm shocked you were this surprised when you knew of my existence in the first place," was the simple answer from Ryan as he folded his arms and bobbed his muscles.

Everything was beginning to make sense to Julia.

"Please, I'm sorry, just let me go; you'll never hear of this from anyone, I promise," she pleaded in tears, only to be met by the roaring laughter from the Bonnie and Clyde of murder.

Julia wondered if she'd cracked an inside joke or if their sense of humor was just plain twisted.

"The Carver is always certain no one will ever hear of his activities; why do you think he'd make another mistake like Martha and put that certainty to chance?" Karen returned to her sight line wearing only an apron and a barber's gear. However, that wasn't what caught Julia's attention;

the locket that dangled between her huge breasts made Julia's eyes widen by a fraction. Maybe there was hope for her after all.

"You're wearing my locket," she stated as Karen closed in on her.

"I know, right?" Karen smiled sweetly. "It's kind of ironic that even though I'm the barber, the Carver's trophies are the sweet, sweet red locks of hair. Although the Carver takes out organs and gives them to me, the proceeds are for our well-being, so I can't keep them as trophies, you see. I only get to keep worthless trinkets from every..."

As Karen yammered on, Julia looked at the wall in the room and saw different sizes of framed Ziploc bags of red hair. She could not count, but there weren't less than fifty Ziploc frames.

Her blood ran cold.

They'd only recovered eight bodies; at least forty-six bodies were nowhere to be found.

When Ryan realized what she was looking at, he could guess her thought process.

"Don't worry about the rest. The only reason you saw those bodies in the forest place was that I wanted to—we wanted to teach Ray a lesson for being a fucking goody-two-shoes all our lives and for trying to kill me. Now that we have him rest assured, your body in such a humiliating manner they're never finding."

He didn't seem like he was joking. That made it all the scarier for Julia.

It was needless to say that she was nearing her end. Unlike her partner, this man who looked so alike was going to kill her without even batting an eyelid, and the only thing she could do was wait and hope that Peter got to where they were as soon as possible.

She sincerely prayed for a miracle to happen, but the only thing the prayer seemed to have yielded was Karen turning on her clippers.

"Let me start by telling you how all this began," Karen spoke as she dug her hands into Julia's hair and pulled at the roots.

Julia could only whimper in pain.

"My love's first heartbreak was served to him by a natural redhead like yourself, his own mother." She began cutting through her hair as Ryan pulled at his belt strings and began to undress. "The woman would always tell him 'no' whenever he asked her for anything. There was never a time she ever said yes to him..."

Ryan's groan caused Julia to look in his direction, and she immediately regretted it. The man was totally naked from the waist down, touching his flaccid penis in response to the mix of the whirring of the clippers and Karen's droning voice.

Julia soon realized she was beginning to drift in and out of consciousness.

"...she always wanted Ray and never Ryan, even in bed. She starved him from her body for so long, forcing herself onto the one who didn't even want her that way..."

Julia's eyes widened to the size of a penny. Ray's mother sleeping with him? "...when Ryan forcefully took what was rightfully his, all hell broke loose..."

It went on and on, and the clippers kept grazing Julia. Her lush, wild mane was scraping off; Ryan kept pumping his penis in reaction to whatever the fuck was arousing him in the entire scene and grunting like a lunatic until the crazed man pumped out his orgasm and then fell to his knees.

It wasn't until his face proceeded to kiss the bloodstained carpet and a sudden yelp came from Karen as she abandoned the clippers and rushed towards him that Julia realized her miracles might just have come in the nick of time to save her.

Even though she wanted to wait long enough to thank her hero, she fell unconscious before they got to her.

Chapter Ten.

For the first eighteen hours after the ordeal, Julia drifted in and out of consciousness.

Dark then light, in and out.

Her vitals went up and down.

Gasping for air and frantically trying to grab something to make it stop.

The feeling she was experiencing felt as if she was on a roller coaster ride of mental torture. The fading in and out gave Julia motion sickness and the feeling of repeatedly dying and being brought back to life. When Julia drifted in for the first time, it was in a hospital room.

The overhead lights were harsh;

her throat felt like it grabbed a high-pitched sandpaper grinder, with the grains slicing like diamonds, and her lips felt like lead from an injection, heavy and limp.

Julia's body felt like she was filled with sand and placed to block water from a flood. However, Julia took solace in the fact that Peter was there, holding her right hand in both of his.

He kept whispering honeyed words into her ears, and she drifted off feeling very safe.

The second time, it wasn't so pleasant. The first person she saw was Ray, but due to her trauma, she thought he was Ryan, the sadistic piece of shit that wanted to end her very existence on this earth, and as a result, her vitals spiked like never before.

The doctors rushed to treat Julia for the abnormal vitals. Ultimately, she had to have administered a sedation medicine to calm her heart rate and lower her blood pressure to normal.

The next time she woke up, the room was empty, and she stared straight at the ceiling for at least ten minutes before slipping back into the dark abyss of unconsciousness. The things Julia saw in her mind while unconscious would make even the sickest animals quiver with fear.

She had envisioned a man standing in the distance in the dark, laughing like a madman walking toward her, holding a long blade with blood dripping off the end.

His footsteps were as clear as the thumping of a heart.

The distortion of the dripping acid background was tormenting her mind with what her reality was.

He started cutting away her body and peeling back the flesh while moaning and giggling. She could feel the blade slicing and cut into her very being, which was taking a toll on her sanity.

Screaming and lashing out for the surrender of her life to just end. The last and final time Julia woke up, awakened from the horrible nightmare;

Ray was in the room again, and he'd been holding her hand even before she jerked awake. The aftermath of the nightmare had her retracting from Ray's hold. Although he let her go and raised his hands in surrender, he also spoke to assure her that he was not who she imagined he was.

"I am not Ryan; I promise." As he talked, she looked right into his eyes to be sure. She finally relaxed when she saw the humanity and sincerity in his eyes.

"You scared the hell out of me," Julia whispered weakly. The relief on her face was visible even to someone a kilometer away.

"Please tell me your evil twin and his sidekick are dead for real this time."

Julia wasn't one to wish death upon people, but she could tell, from the very brief encounter she had with Ryan and Karen, that they were people whose only remedy for their mental illness was death.

"Karen is safely behind bars, but I made sure to kill Ryan at the scene. Undoubtedly, I wish he lived enough for me to certainly give him a little dose of the torture he'd served so many women. His accomplice will certainly be facing the death sentence too." Ray looked very intense as he made his speech. He seemed like he regretted his twin's easy death.

There was silence in the hospital room for a moment. Julia spent time ruminating over the happenings of the day before, and an involuntary shiver went crawling down her spine when she realized how close Ray was to a death row sentence for a crime he didn't even commit.

She wondered how the twin had masterminded the entire scenario to fit into Ray's schedule, thereby incriminating him. Even to the point of DNA matches, he'd perfectly set up a special agent to dot the 'i' and cross the 't.' "He would have been a genius if he wasn't so evil," Julia concluded aloud, and Ray hummed in response.

"I am so sorry about your hair," Ray tenderly whispered as he looked at her bandaged head. "It looked stunning on you, but you're still gorgeous nevertheless."

"Acknowledged." Julia nodded and smiled, even though the latter didn't reach her eyes. "I've always wanted to try something new anyways. It gives me the perfect opportunity."

Ray nodded, and then silence engulfed the air once again. This time the silence made the awkwardness in the air more noticeable.

"How did you find me?" Julia questioned to make conversation. She already knew her locket had done a chunk of the work.

However, she was low-key, curious as to how and why Peter had let him out to chase after his brother.

"When McCain came calling, I told the sheriff about my twin brother, our tumultuous childhood, and how I suspected he hadn't really died as the reports had said. Even though all the evidence was against me, I found enough evidence for McCain to believe me. The biggest one was how you'd soon switch on your tracking chip if you had not already done so.

"We tracked you to the apartment beside the one I'd been leasing. It turned out they leased me the apartment to fit into their plans. Karen knew my boss Liz and had done her a few favors in the past; Karen asked for me to come home, which qualified me for the case.

"According to Karen's confession statement, she had been planning the entire thing for about three years with my twin to take the fall for every kill they'd ever made. A whopping three hundred and twenty-two in the span of their fifteen years together"

Julia knew there'd been a lot of victims. Still, over three hundred? God, this duo were monsters.

"...they were mostly women from the neighboring cities. They disposed of them after harvesting their organs in awfully creative ways. I really cannot tell you for obvious reasons.

We found you in the attic of the apartment next door to mine, and I took Ryan down from a far range while Peter and his boys utilized Karen's distraction to infiltrate the building. The rest is history."

The silence in the air was pregnant with rumination. Julia tried to process the entirety of all she'd learned since she woke up.. Still, exhaustion began to overtake her.

"There was something very striking I heard. At the same time, in the process of getting a shave," "If you don't mind my asking?" "I'd like to know if it's true that—"

"My mom sexually abused me while Ryan paid me back with interest?" Ray interrupted Julia's question with one of his own. When Julia nodded to ascertain that it was all she wanted to know, he mirrored her action, and Julia sighed in exhaustion.

"That must have been a very tough childhood," she said solemnly. "It was, but I pulled through and made meaning out of my life." Ray shrugged along with his answer.

"Sadly, Ryan was unable to do the same—"

"You can't blame that on his past, Jules. You've had it worse than the both of us combined, but you moved past it and made a meaningful future for yourself. He should have done better. I kept taking up punishments for his crimes because he promised to do better, but he just grew into a narcissistic, entitled prick who played God over people's lives because they refused him at one point or another. I'm not happy he turned out this way, trust me, but I cannot say I regret killing him. The only regret I ever regretted was that I didn't kill him fifteen years ago."

Even though all Ray said was true, Julia was sorrowful that such a genius became infected with madness because of a traumatic childhood and wasted many lives in the end. It was truly very sad.

If only he had a better understanding of life.

"So what's next for you, Mr. Rivera?" Julia's eyes snapped up at the sound of her "father," His smile towards her told the tale of his love and gratitude that she had made it through.

"I'll receive a promotion at the bureau if Liz gets prosecuted for her involvement in organ trafficking."

Ray was struggling and thinking he had almost made the gravest mistake of his life because he believed Liz wanted to have a relationship with him. Still, she assigned Ray to the case because she was working with Ryan to end Ray's life and career. Ray feels devastated by the whole plan and Liz, his great "crush." Ray's stomach turns, and he feels disgusted with himself for being so taken in by such an evil woman.

Ray was clearing his throat to mask his emotions.

"I might resign, settle here, and practice from a private agency; I'm undecided at the moment."

"Well, you can include working at the department as an option if you want? We would be honored to accept you on our team," Peter offered warmly. Still, Ray shook his head with a playful wince.

"I don't think the PD can afford to have a special agent at their beck and call, with all due respect, sir."

McCain chuckled heartily at the response, and Ray smirked. Both men looked like they were moving on from the horrific experience of the past few weeks in culmination.

However, Julia knew it would take a lot of therapy and antidepressants to keep her mind from snapping like a bent twig under the weight of all the new information she'd just heard.

She was still even scared to ask if Troyer had made it out alive or if Ray's evil twin had succeeded in murdering him too. If the happenings in her latest nightmare were trusted enough to go by, he'd also met a gruesome end.

Maybe this would have been the perfect ending for so many, making it out of the den of a serial killer alive, that is. But to Julia, it was just the beginning of a nightmare.

Don't miss out!

Visit the website below and you can sign up to receive emails whenever Jason Morgan publishes a new book. There's no charge and no obligation.

https://books2read.com/r/B-A-ZFFV-TDMBC

BOOKS2READ

Connecting independent readers to independent writers.

About the Author

Jason Morgan can't get enough of psychological thrillers. His novellas are edge-of-your-seat good. But that's not all Jason enjoys – he also loves music, cooking, collecting comics (including Funko Pops), and spending time outdoors with family and friends.

Read more at https://www.facebook.com/PsychologicallyThrilling.